# Rapunzel
### and
# Rumpelstiltskin

*For Siân*
*P.B.*

Orchard Books
96 Leonard Street, London EC2A 4XD
*Orchard Books Australia*
Unit 31/56 O'Riordan Street, Alexandria, NSW 2015
The text was first published in Great Britain in the form
of a gift collection called *The Orchard Book of Fairy Tales*,
illustrated by Ian Beck, in 1992
This edition first published in hardback in 2000
First paperback publication in 2001
Text © Rose Impey 1992
Illustrations © Peter Bailey 2000
The rights of Rose Impey to be identified as the author
and Peter Bailey to be identified as the illustrator have
been asserted by them in accordance with the
Copyright, Designs and Patents Act, 1988.
A CIP catalogue record for this book is available from the British Library
ISBN 1 84121 570 8 (hardback)
ISBN 1 84121 576 7 (paperback)
1 2 3 4 5 6 7 8 9 10 (hardback)
1 2 3 4 5 6 7 8 9 10 (paperback)
Printed in Great Britain

# Rapunzel
### and
# Rumpelstiltskin

### Retold by Rose Impey
### Illustrated by Peter Bailey

 ORCHARD BOOKS

# Rapunzel

It is a hard thing to want a child and never to have one. There was once a couple who had all but given up hope when at last the wife became pregnant and it seemed as if their prayers had been answered.

As the months passed, the woman spent many hours sitting at her bedroom window, which overlooked a neighbouring garden. It was full of fine vegetables and beautiful flowers, but it was entirely surrounded by a high wall to keep out trespassers. The garden belonged to a powerful witch, and everyone was afraid of her.

One summer's day, as the woman looked down on the lush green vegetables, her gaze fell on a bed of delicious rapunzel plants.

They looked so tempting that the woman couldn't keep her eyes off them. Oh, what she would give for a taste of them!

Soon she had a craving for the plant, which is sometimes the way with pregnant women. She wouldn't eat anything else. She began to look pale and weak.

"What's wrong, my dear?" asked her husband, who hated to see her unhappy.

"I must have some of that rapunzel," she told him, "otherwise I think I might die."

Now the man was in a dilemma. He couldn't see his wife waste away for the sake of a few rapunzel plants. But the thought of stealing into that forbidden garden chilled his heart. At last, however, it was clear he had no choice.

Late one night the man climbed the high wall and dropped silently to the ground. He crept through the vegetable plot and snatched a handful of plants, then stole away with them, his heart beating fast.

When she saw the rapunzel his wife fell upon it and ate it as if she hadn't eaten for a week, which was almost the case.

But even then she wasn't satisfied. She must have more. Nothing else would do.

So the next night the poor man had to go again. Imagine his horror this time when he dropped cat-like from the wall to find the witch there, waiting for him.

"Now I've caught you," she said. "Steal from me, would you? You'll live to regret this."

Spare me, please have mercy. I'm not really a thief. I only came out of desperation, to save my wife, who is pregnant. Without your rapunzel plants I thought she would die."

When the witch heard this she changed her tune entirely.

"Why, help yourself. Take as much as you want. Come as often as you like."

For a moment the man looked relieved, until he heard what else she had to say.

"But in exchange you must give me the baby when it is born."

Then the man looked distraught. What kind of exchange was that?

"Don't worry," said the witch, "I'll love the child and care for it like a mother. Come now, what do you say?"

What could he say? The poor man was terrified of the witch, and before he knew what had happened he had promised the baby to her. Then there was no going back.

When it was time, the woman gave birth to a little girl, and soon the witch came to claim her. No amount of pleading could persuade the witch to leave the child. The couple had made

their bargain; now they must stick to it.
The witch named her Rapunzel after the
plants that caused the trouble, and took
the child away to live with her.

The girl grew very beautiful, strong
and healthy, with long hair the colour
of molten gold that fell like a river
way past her waist. The witch kept her
word; she did care for the girl, and
loved her like a mother.

When Rapunzel reached twelve she was so beautiful that the witch couldn't bear to share her with anyone. She took the girl to live in a high tower in the middle of a wood. It had neither a door nor a staircase, only a window at the very top, so that no one else could ever reach her.

Each day, when the witch visited, she would stand below the girl's window and call out:

*"Rapunzel, Rapunzel, let down your hair."*

Then the girl, whose hair was longer than ever, wrapped it twice around a window hook and lowered it more than twenty yards to the ground, and the witch climbed up, as if it were a ladder.

In this way Rapunzel's lonely life went on for several years. The girl wasn't happy, but she wasn't exactly unhappy either.

One day, quite by chance, a young prince was riding in the woods when he heard a sweet voice carried on the air. It was Rapunzel, singing to keep herself company. Following the sound, he discovered the tall tower, but he could find no way inside and at last, discouraged, he rode home.

The prince could think of nothing except the beautiful voice and he returned day after day to listen to her singing.

As he stood in the shade of a tree one day, he saw a wizened old woman approach the tower and call out in a rusty voice:

*"Rapunzel, Rapunzel, let down your hair."*

Then a mass of golden hair tumbled down and the witch climbed up it.

"If that's the way to the sweet bird's nest," thought the prince, "I shall climb the ladder too."

The next day, around dusk, the prince called out:

*"Rapunzel, Rapunzel, let down your hair,"*

And the hair fell down like a waterfall, and the prince climbed up.

When she saw that her visitor was a young man, instead of the witch, Rapunzel was afraid. Locked away in her tower she knew nothing of men. But when the prince spoke softly and looked at her so gently, she knew she could trust him.

"Once I had heard your voice I couldn't rest until I saw you," he told her. "Now I cannot rest until you promise to marry me."

Rapunzel thought how handsome he was and how much happier she would be with him than with the witch. She  took his hand and agreed to marry him.

But how would it be possible to escape, imprisoned as she was in this tower? She would weave a ladder, not of hair, but of silk, which the prince would bring, each time he visited her.

"Be sure to come at night," she told him. "The witch visits by day and she must never see you."

So the prince took care always to come at night, and that way the witch suspected nothing. But at last Rapunzel gave herself away.

"Why is it," she asked the witch one day, "that you are so much heavier to pull up than the prince? He climbs up in a…" Too late! She could have bitten off her tongue. "Oh, treacherous girl," screamed the witch. "You have deceived me."

She snatched up a pair of scissors in one hand and Rapunzel's beautiful hair in the other, and snip! snap! in a moment it lay on the floor.

Even then she showed no mercy.

She turned the girl out of the tower and left her in a wild and desolate place to fend for herself as best she could.

Later that same day, when the prince came and called out: *"Rapunzel, Rapunzel, let down your hair,"* The witch cunningly tied the golden hair to the window hook and lowered it down.

The prince climbed up quickly and found, to his horror, not the sweet Rapunzel, but the wizened old woman looking at him with poisonous eyes.

"So you thought you would steal the songbird, did you? Well, the cat's got her and the cat'll get you too. She's gone, and you'll never see her again," she gloated.

Half mad with grief, the prince threw himself from the tower and would have died had he not landed in the thickest briars. But although he survived, thorns pierced his eyes and blinded him.

For many years he wandered through the woods living on whatever he could find, grieving for his lost wife, Rapunzel. Eventually he wandered through the same wilderness where Rapunzel was living, with barely enough food for herself and the twins she had borne.

Just as he had done so long ago, the prince heard a sweet voice coming through the trees. It was a voice he knew, and he made his way towards it. Rapunzel saw him, and recognising him, threw her arms around him, weeping tears of joy and sorrow. Two drops falling on his eyes healed them and restored his sight.

Then the two were united again and
the prince took Rapunzel and their
children back to his own kingdom. At
last, they could all live happily ever after.

# Rumpelstiltskin

Now this story is about a poor miller who never knows when to hold his tongue; it's always getting him into bother. This miller has a daughter, pretty as a picture, and clever – she has brains enough for the pair of them. He's forever boasting about all the things she can do, but one time he goes too far, and this is how it happens.

The miller has some business with the king and when it's done he soon gets round to his favourite subject.

He says to the king, "I have a daughter, Your Majesty, such a beauty she puts the sun to shame."

Now the king's hardly likely to be interested in the miller's daughter; he's already bored.

"And clever," says the miller, "there's nothing my daughter can't do."

The king yawns. The miller's desperate to impress him.

"Why, she can even...spin straw into gold," says he.

*Spin straw into gold!* Now the king's listening; he's all ears. This king loves gold more than anything in the world. He can't get enough of it.

He says to the miller, "I'd like to meet your daughter. Send her to the palace. We'll see if she can really do as you say. But I warn you, if you've lied to me, she'll lose her head."

So the miller goes home and tells his daughter what he's done.

"Oh, Father!" says the girl. "That's a fine mess you've got me into. You and your big mouth. Now what'll I do?"

Well what can she do? When a king says do a thing, you best do it; nobody argues with a king. So the girl puts on her smartest clothes and takes herself off to the palace.

When she gets there the king shows the girl into a large room. There's nothing in it but a stool, a spinning wheel and stacks and stacks of straw.

"Now," says he, "let's see you spin this straw into gold by morning or else it'll be off with your head."

And he locks the door and leaves her there.

The girl may be clever, but she isn't that clever. She doesn't know *what* to do so she stamps her feet and throws her apron over her head. She howls, more out of frustration than fear.

When she finally stops to draw breath she hears a scritch, scratching noise at the window. Up she gets and opens it and in leaps a little wee man. He's got eyes like pieces of coal and dangly legs and his hands look just itching to pinch something. And all the while he's grinning.

"What's up with you?" says he.

"What's it to you?" says she.

"Don't hurt to tell," says he.

"S'ppose it don't," says she. And she tells him the whole story, first and last, and then she bursts out crying again.

"And it can't be done," says she.

"I can do it," says he. "You watch me."

The girl looks at him, to see if he's serious.

"What'll it cost?" says she, suspicious-like.

"That necklace'll do," says he, reaching out his little grabby hand. So the girl gives it him. There and then he sits himself down on the stool and he's off.

Whirl, whirl, whirl, three times round and the bobbin's full of shining gold thread. Then whirl, whirl, whirl, and there's another one. As easy as that. No matter how close the girl watches she can't see the trick of it.

In the end she lies down on a small heap in the straw and sleeps while the little wee man does all the work for her. When she wakes he's gone and the room's bright with shining gold.

Come morning, the king unlocks the door and he's highly delighted. He takes one look at the gold and he wants more. He leads the girl to an even bigger room with stacks and stacks and stacks of straw.

"Well, you've done it once," he says, "let's see you do it again. Spin all this straw into gold by morning – if you want to keep that pretty head of yours."

And he locks the door and takes away the key.

She doesn't know what to do. She's been lucky once, but a second time... She sits and stares at the straw.

After a time – a long time, a short time, who knows how long she sits staring – the girl hears the same scritch, scratching sound at the window.

Well, up she jumps and lets in that little wee man. He stands there grinning. *He* can see what *she's* thinking, and she can read his mind equally well.

"I've only got this ring left," says she.

"That'll do," says he, plucking it off her finger.

Then down he sits and he's off.

Whirl, whirl, whirl, three times round and the bobbin's full. The girl lies down and the sound of the wheel, whirl, whirl, whirl, soon lulls her to sleep.

When she wakes it's as if the sun's come inside the room, it makes her eyes ache to look at it. The king arrives and his eyes fair pop out. He looks at the girl and he thinks, 'She's only a miller's daughter but she's right pretty and she's already made me very rich.'

But the man's greedy, oh he's greedy, all right.

This time he leads her to a great barn of a room that's so full of straw she can hardly fit through the door.

"Now, my dear," says he, "if you can spin this straw into gold I'll make you my wife. But if you can't, well..."

He doesn't need to spell it out. By now she knows what it will cost her. The girl sits down totally at a loss. Even suppose the little wee man comes again, he won't help her for nothing – and nothing's all she's got left to give him.

Sure enough she hears his fingers scritch, scratching at the window. She ups and opens it and in he comes, grinning as usual. His bony little shoulders are shaking, he's that pleased with himself.

"Before you ask," says she, "I've nothing left to give you. And that's the truth."

But the little wee man says, "I can still help you – if you'll promise me your firstborn child."

'Child!' thinks the girl. 'I'm not even married yet.'

That's far off in the future, she'll worry about that when and if it happens. For now she has herself to think about.

"All right," says she, "only do hurry up."

There's that much straw this time she's worried he'll not be done by morning. But the little wee man sets to work and spins faster than ever, so fast it makes her dizzy to watch. Whirl, whirl, whirl, like a whirlwind.

When the king comes in the next day he looks like the cat that got the cream. He's found himself a real beauty for a wife and now he has more gold than he could have dreamed of.

True to his word, the pair are straightaway married. They live happily enough for over a year. They have a bonny little baby that they dote on.

The queen's clean forgot the promise she made, and she's forgot all about the little wee man. That's convenient isn't it?

But promises have a way of coming back to haunt you. When the baby's just old enough to have worked his way into her heart the queen has a visitor, and not a welcome one neither. The little wee man suddenly appears in her room.

"That child's mine," says he. "Hand him over."

But the queen'd die first. She clutches the baby to her. She'd swallow him to keep him safe.

"You're not having him," says she. "I'll give you anything else." She offers him a horse, a house, a palace…the entire riches of the kingdom – but that don't work.

"Riches are nothing to me. It's that babby I want. Come on, a promise is a promise."

Then the queen sets up crying. She howls and she sobs, she weeps and she wails, as if her heart'll break. Such a carry-on, and lucky for her it seems to work.

"All right, all right, all right," says the little wee man. He can't a-bear the sound of crying. "I'll tell you what I'll do. I'll give you three days to come up with my name. If you manage it you can keep him. But don't build up your hopes," says he. And he stretches out his poky little hand towards the baby. The queen snatches him away.

The little wee man sneers and says, "Guess me in nine or that babby's mine." And off he goes, fair puffed up with conceit.

Well the poor queen never sleeps that night. She sits up making lists and lists of all the names she can think of. Next morning she sends messengers off, up and down the country, to see what they can find. It won't be an ordinary name, that much she knows.

At dusk when the little wee man appears at the window the queen's ready for him.

"Now," says he, "have you guessed my name?"

"Is it Nehemiah?" says she.

"No, it's not," says he.

"Is it Obadiah?" says she.

"No, it's not," says he.

"Then it must be Zachariah," says she.

"Oh, no, it's not that neither," says he, and he grins fit to split his face. And away he goes triumphant. So that's one chance she's lost.

The second day the queen asks everyone around but the more names she collects the harder it is to choose. She starts to think of all the names she'd *like* to call him.

That night when he comes he says, "All right, what's my name?"

"Is it Hornyhands?" says she.

"No it's not," says he, although it could have been.

"Is it Skinnyshanks?" says she.

"No it's not," says he. But that would've suited him too.

"Well is it Grinningidiot?" says she.

"Oh, no, it's not," says he, grinning even harder.

He looks at her with eyes like burning coals and he says, "Only tomorrow and that babby's mine. Three more'll make nine, then he's mine, mine, mine."

Off he goes, laughing and shrieking. And that's her second chance gone.

Then it's the third day. She's all but given up hope when the last of her messengers returns. He's got no new names for her but he does have a strange story to tell.

As he was making his way home he passed through a wood and in a clearing he spied a weird little man dancing round a fire and singing to himself:

*"Tonight I brew, tonight I bake,*
*Tomorrow the Queen's*
*little babby I take.*
*She can't win this*
*little game,*
*For Rumpelstiltskin*
*is my name."*

Well, when she hears this the queen's fit to burst with excitement. She can't wait for the little man to come that night. When she opens the window, in he leaps and ooh, he looks so pleased with himself. His little black eyes are shining and he's wriggling, as if his body won't keep still. The queen pretends to be real scared of him.

"Now, then, my lovely, what's my name?" says he.

"Ermm, is it Abberdabber?" says she.

"No, it's not," says he, and he comes a little closer.

"Oh dear, is it Bobanob?" says she.

"No, it's not," says he, coming even closer and grinning from ear to ear. Then he points his bony finger at her and says, "Take your time, my beauty. One more guess and that babby's mine."

He's close enough now to reach out and touch the baby.

So the queen steps back
a little and then she
breaks out grinning too.
"Well, could it
be Rumplestiltskin
by any chance?"
The little wee man
shrieks, "Who told you! Who told you?
The devil must have told you."

Then BANG! he
stamps so hard his
right leg disappears
into the floor.

Then BANG! he
stamps his other
leg and that
goes down too.

Then whoosh! right through the hole and he keeps on going, down, down, down into the ground until he's clean disappeared. All that's left is the hole.

And as sure as five and five make ten, nobody ever saw *him* again. And that's a true story, or my name isn't...

# HANS CHRISTIAN ANDERSEN TALES FROM ORCHARD BOOKS

## RETOLD BY ANDREW MATTHEWS
## ILLUSTRATED BY PETER BAILEY

1 **The Emperor's New Clothes and The Tinder Box**
  1 84121 663 1          £3.99

2 **The Little Match Girl and The Wild Swans**
  1 84121 675 5          £3.99

3 **The Little Mermaid and The Princess and the Pea**
  1 84121 667 4          £3.99

4 **Thumbelina and The Tin Soldier**
  1 84121 671 2          £3.99

Orchard Fairy Tales are available from all good bookshops,
or can be ordered direct from the publisher:
Orchard Books, PO BOX 29, Douglas IM99 1BQ
Credit card orders please telephone 01624 836000
or fax 01624 837033
or e-mail: bookshop@enterprise.net for details.

To order please quote title, author and ISBN
and your full name and address.
Cheques and postal orders should be
made payable to 'Bookpost plc'.
Postage and packing is FREE within the UK
(overseas customers should add £1.00 per book).

Prices and availability are subject to change.